BOSSY BEAR
at the CIRCUS

BY JUNE WOODMAN

ILLUSTRATED BY PAMELA STOREY·

GONDOLA

The circus is in town!
Bossy Bear loves the circus.
He runs to tell his friend,
Hoppy Rabbit.
"The circus is in town!"
says Bossy.
"I love the circus," says
Hoppy. "Come on,
we must go."
They get into Hoppy's car
and off they go.

They stop at Paddy Dog's house. He is outside.

"The circus is in town!" say Bossy and Hoppy.

"I love the circus," says Paddy. "I want to go too."

"Hop into the car," says Hoppy Rabbit.

Paddy gets into the car and off they go.

They stop at the duck pond.
Dilly Duck and her three
ducklings are there with Merry
Mole and Flippy Frog.
"The circus is in town!" say
Bossy and Hoppy and Paddy.
"We love the circus. We want
to go too," say the three
little ducklings.
"Hop into the car," says
Hoppy Rabbit.
They all get into the car
and off they go.

Soon they get to the big circus tent. They go inside. Then the circus begins. "Look, here come the lions!" says Hoppy Rabbit. The lions do lots of tricks. "I can do tricks too," says Bossy Bear. "Look at me!" He runs into the circus ring.

But the lions are cross with Bossy. They hit him with their big paws and he falls down. BUMP!
"Oh! Oh! Stop it!" says Bossy. The lions roar at him and Bossy Bear runs away.
"He is very funny," say Merry Mole and Flippy Frog.
"He is very SILLY!" says Dilly Duck.

"Here come the sea lions!"
says Paddy Dog.
The sea lions are very clever.
They do lots of tricks.
"I can do tricks too," says
Bossy Bear. "Look at me!"
He goes into the circus ring
with the sea lions. He takes
a big blue ball and puts it
on his nose.

But the sea lions are cross with Bossy. They want the blue ball back. They slap him with their flippers and throw wet fish at him.
"Oh! Oh! Stop it!" says Bossy. He runs out of the ring.
The sea lions move after him.
"Bossy is funny," say Merry Mole and Flippy Frog.

"Look at the elephants!"
says Dilly to her ducklings.
The elephants go round the
circus ring. Each one holds
on to the next one's tail.
Last of all comes a little
baby elephant.
"I love the baby elephant,"
says Cuddly Cat.

Bossy runs into the ring
and pulls the tail of the
baby elephant.
"Look at me!" says Bossy
Bear.
But the baby elephant is
very cross. It slaps Bossy
with its trunk.
Bossy Bear falls down.
BUMP!
"Bossy is very funny," say
the three little ducklings.

"Look, here come the clowns!"
they all say. The clowns run
into the ring. They have
a bucket of water and a big
bucket of paste. They can do
very clever tricks. They do
not get wet. They do not
get sticky.
"I can do tricks too!"
says Bossy Bear.

"Come here, Bossy," say the clowns. "Come and be the new circus clown."
They give him a funny hat and big black boots. Then they give him a big red nose.
"Here is a funny new clown!" they all say.
"Look at me!" says Bossy Bear.

Bossy can do some tricks, but he is not so clever. His boots are much too big for him and he falls over.
BUMP!
He falls into the bucket of water. Then he falls into the bucket of paste.
Poor Bossy is very wet and very sticky.
But he does look funny!

"Stay and be a clown, Bossy,"
say the other clowns.
"Oh no, Bossy!" says Cuddly.
"Oh no, Bossy!" says Dilly.
Bossy is very wet and sticky.
He is very cross too.
"No!" says Bossy. "The circus
is no fun for a clown. I think
I will just be Bossy Bear!"

Say these words again

sticky	last
flippers	baby
paws	tail
roars	trunk
blue	bucket
throws	water
slaps	paste